Jan 20

The Masterpiece Adventures BOOK FOUR

MARVIN & JAMES

SAVE THE DAY!

and Elaine helps!

ELISE BROACH

Illustrated by

KELLY MURPHY

Christy Ottaviano Books

Henry Holt and Company • NEW YORK

Henry Holt and Company, *Publishers since 1866*
175 Fifth Avenue, New York, NY 10010
mackids.com

Henry Holt® is a registered trademark of Macmillan Publishing Group, LLC
Text copyright © 2019 by Elise Broach
Illustrations copyright © 2019 by Kelly Murphy
All rights reserved.

Our books may be purchased in bulk for promotional, educational, or business use. Please contact your local bookseller or the Macmillan Corporate and Premium Sales Department at (800) 221-7945 ext. 5442 or by email at MacmillanSpecialMarkets@macmillan.com.

Library of Congress Cataloging-in-Publication Data
Names: Broach, Elise, author. I Murphy, Kelly, 1977– illustrator.
Title: Marvin & James save the day (and Elaine helps!) /
Elise Broach ; illustrated by Kelly Murphy.
Other titles: Marvin and James save the day (and Elaine helps!)
Description: First edition. I New York : Henry Holt and Company, 2019. I Series: The masterpiece adventures ; book 4 I "Christy Ottaviano Books." I Summary: Marvin the beetle tries to reassure his human boy, James, who is worried about his father's upcoming wedding and the changes it will bring.
Identifiers: LCCN 2018021058 I ISBN 9781250186072 (hardcover)
Subjects: I CYAC: Weddings—Fiction. I Beetles—Fiction. I Human–animal relationships—Fiction. I Friendship—Fiction.
Classification: LCC PZ7.B78083 Mar 2019 I DDC [Fic]—dc23
LC record available at https://lccn.loc.gov/2018021058

First edition, 2019 / Designed by April Ward and Sophie Erb
The artist used pen and ink on Coventry Rag paper
to create the illustrations for this book.
Printed in the United States of America by
LSC Communications, Harrisonburg, Virginia
1   3   5   7   9   10   8   6   4   2

For my wonderful nieces and goddaughters,
Julia Elise Broach and Jane Solan Urheim,
in honor of our many conversations about love

—E. B.

For Tammie, with love and thanks

—K. M.

Contents

CHAPTER ONE

Big News

Marvin is so excited that he runs in circles on James's desk. Karl and Christina are coming to visit! Karl is James's father, an artist just like Marvin, except that he doesn't draw tiny pictures. He paints giant ones, full of color. Christina is Karl's girlfriend and James's friend,

and Marvin likes her very much. She works at the Metropolitan Museum of Art. Marvin thinks the Met is the best museum in the whole world.

Karl and Christina see James often, but today, they are coming because they have *big news*. What could it be?

"Maybe they're getting a dog!"
James says.

James would love a dog. But he
lives with his mother and stepfather,
Mr. and Mrs. Pompaday, and no dogs
are allowed in their apartment.

Marvin races across the desk to
a picture he once made for James, a
drawing of the beach. He taps it with
two of his legs.

"Oh!" James says. "Do you think they'll take me to the beach?"

Marvin does not want James to go away, but it's fun to think about a trip to the beach.

"I have an idea," says James. "Maybe my dad is getting a new car."

He takes a little toy car from his shelf and zooms it across the desk.

Marvin watches it fly past.

"Hey," James says. "Want a ride?"

Before Marvin has time to think, James picks him up and puts him in the front seat of the tiny car.

Marvin is in the driver's seat! He puts his front legs on the steering wheel.

James taps the car with his finger. *Whoosh!*

It speeds across the desk.

Marvin is driving!

James laughs. "Now you're a race-car driver."

Why didn't they ever do this before? Marvin loves riding in the car. It is so fast, much faster than crawling.

"Let's put it on the floor," James says. James and Marvin race the car across the bedroom rug over and over again, with Marvin driving.

Once, it bangs into the leg of the chair.

Bump!

Marvin almost falls out.

But the rest of the time, the car goes very fast in a straight line. Marvin thinks he is an excellent driver. He wishes his cousin, Elaine, could see how fast he's going.

"Wouldn't it be cool if my dad got a new car?" James says.

They are just thinking how great this would be when they hear a knock on James's door.

Karl and Christina are standing there, smiling.

Marvin sees their happy faces
and has a sudden feeling that the
big news is not a dog or a trip to the
beach or a race car.

"James," Karl says, bending down
with his arms out. "We have
something to tell you."

Christina hugs James too, as they say in one loud, excited voice: "We're getting married!"

James looks at them with wide eyes. "Wow," he says.

Marvin slips out of the tiny car and crawls behind it so nobody will see him.

"Isn't it fantastic?" Karl asks.

"We're so happy," Christina says. "Are you happy?"

"Yes," James says quickly. "That's great."

Marvin is watching James. He thinks that James does not look very happy. He certainly doesn't look as happy as Karl and Christina.

But why not? James loves Christina. Marvin knows that.

"The wedding is going to be at the Cloisters," Christina tells James. "Have you ever been to the Cloisters?"

James shakes his head.

"It's a very old church that was moved here, stone by stone, from France."

"Really?" James says. "Across the ocean?"

This sounds strange to
Marvin. But he has learned that
humans sometimes do the strangest
things.

"Yes," Christina tells him. "It's part
of the museum, even though it's a
few miles away. The Cloisters has
some of the Met's art from the
Middle Ages."

"And it will be a nice place for a wedding," Karl says. "It's high on a cliff above the Hudson River."

"Cool," James says.

Marvin thinks James seems especially quiet.

"I know this is a lot to take in, buddy," Karl says. "But I have one more thing to tell you . . . or ask you, really."

"What?" James looks up at Karl.

Marvin peeks over the top of the shiny little car. What more could they possibly say? Isn't this wedding news enough?

Karl takes a deep breath. "I was wondering if you would be my best man?"

"You mean . . ." James begins.

"Yes!" Karl says. "You'll stand beside me at the wedding and pass the ring to me when it's time."

Marvin thinks James looks worried.

"It's the most important job at the wedding," Karl says.

Christina nods. "And we want you to do it because you're the most important person in the world to both of us."

Their faces are so full of joy,
Marvin can only hope James will say
yes.

"What do you think, buddy? Can
you do that?" Karl asks.

"Okay," James says.

"Terrific!" Karl hugs him hard.

Christina kisses his cheek. "Oh,
thank you, James. It means so much
to us."

"We have to go," Karl says. "We'll come back later and take you shopping for a suit."

"There's a lot to do," Christina adds. "The wedding is two weeks from Saturday."

Two weeks! Marvin thinks that is very soon.

They hurry off, leaving Marvin and
James alone in the quiet
bedroom.

CHAPTER TWO
So Many Questions

James lies down on the floor.
Marvin can tell they are finished
racing cars.

He crawls close to James's face.

"It's okay," James says.

Marvin waits.

After a minute, James says, "Christina is the best. If my dad has to marry anyone, I'm glad it's her."

Marvin completely agrees. So why does James look sad?

James sighs.

He gently picks up Marvin.

"Let's draw something," he says.

Marvin always loves drawing. But he's surprised that James wants to draw right now.

James puts Marvin on his desk and takes out some paper. Then he opens the bottle of ink and pours a little into the cap, next to Marvin.

Marvin dips his front legs in the ink and makes a swirl at the top of the paper, like this:

James draws at the bottom of the paper.

"I just like things the way they are," he says.

Marvin can certainly understand that. Mama and Papa recently got rid of his bottle-cap swimming pool because it started leaking. They have promised to find Marvin a new swimming pool, but he liked the old one, and he misses it.

James stops drawing. "Is Christina going to move in with my dad?"

Marvin hadn't thought about this. Of course Karl and Christina will live together after they get married.

"Or is my dad going to move in with her?" James asks.

Now Marvin stops drawing too. He can see the worried look on James's face.

"Her place isn't very big. Do you think there will be room for me?" James asks.

So many questions! Marvin wants to tell James that everything will be okay. But there is no way to know that it will be.

James sighs again. He looks at Marvin's inky swirls.

"Hey," he says, pointing to one. "That looks like the top of a tree."

Carefully, James draws the trunk of the tree, and then more trunks, making a forest.

"My dad seems really happy," James says. He draws two people

holding hands. "So does Christina."
Marvin draws more swirls. James
draws a square. At first, Marvin thinks
it is a house. But then James puts a
cross on it, like this:

So Marvin knows it's a church.

Marvin dips his front legs in the ink again. Above the heads of the two people, he draws a heart.

James smiles at Marvin. "Look,"

he says. "They're getting married. Wait, I have an idea." He folds the paper in half and writes on it before showing it to Marvin.

"We made a card for them,"
he says.

Marvin beams up at him. James
is so kind. Even when he is worried
about his whole life changing, he
can't help being nice.

CHAPTER THREE
Wedding Plans

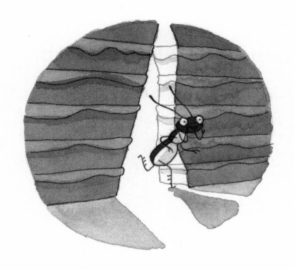

Marvin crawls back to his home under the kitchen sink, eager to share the news.

"Mama! Papa!" he cries. "Where are you?"

They race into the living room, looking alarmed.

"What is it?" Mama asks. "Did you hurt yourself?"

"No, but guess what?" Marvin says. "Karl and Christina are getting married!"

Mama claps her front legs together. "How wonderful!"

Elaine rushes in. "What's going on? What's wonderful?"

So Marvin tells her, and Elaine jumps up and down. "Oh! They're in LOVE!" She covers her heart. "A wedding! Marvin—we have to go."

"Certainly not," Mama says briskly. "Beetles do not belong at a human wedding."

"Karl and Christina don't even know about us," Papa adds. "It's too risky."

"We'll stay out of sight," Elaine says. "Nobody will know. Just think, a real wedding!"

"Now, Elaine," Mama says. "Don't start making plans."

Elaine dances in circles. "We're going to a wedding! James must be so excited. Is he, Marvin? Is he?"

Mama, Papa, and Elaine all look at
Marvin, waiting for his answer.

"Well, not really," he says slowly.

"What? Why not?" Elaine
demands.

"I thought James liked Christina,"
Papa says.

"He does," Marvin says. "I think he's
just . . . worried."

"Worried?" Elaine looks shocked.

But Mama understands. "Of course he is," she says. "It's a big change, for everyone."

Marvin sighs. Poor James.

"But that doesn't mean it won't be a change for the better," Mama says. "James just needs time to get used to it."

The wedding is only two weeks away, Marvin thinks. That isn't a lot of time.

"I know!" Elaine says. "Let's pick out a present for him, from the treasure box. That will cheer him up."

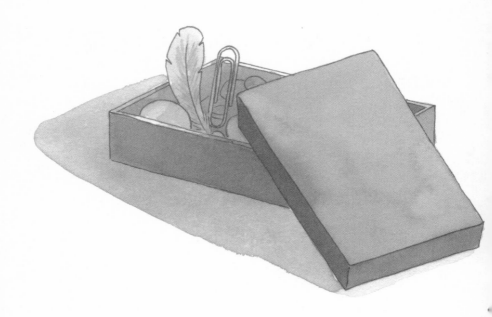

Marvin has to admit this is a good idea. The beetles keep a little box of things they have found in the Pompadays' apartment that are special or pretty but not useful in the beetles' world. This is where Marvin got the buffalo nickel he

gave James as a gift, months ago,
on his birthday.

Elaine races to the treasure box, with
Marvin close behind her.

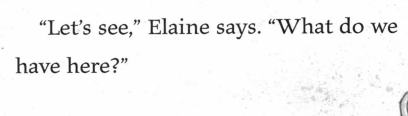

"Let's see," Elaine says. "What do we have here?"

There's a pearl earring,
shiny and white.

There's a bobby pin.

There's a tiny plastic bottle of perfume.

None of these seem like good presents for James.

Marvin and Elaine dig through the
pile of stuff.

"What about this?" Elaine asks. "Isn't it pretty?"

She points to a marble. It's made of glass, pink like a sunset.

But Marvin does not think James needs a marble.

Then Marvin spots a rubber ball.
A super ball!

"This is perfect for James," he tells
Elaine.

"Yay! That will be easy to roll to his
room," she says.

Marvin and Elaine wait until
there is nobody in the kitchen. Then
they roll the super ball out of the
kitchen cupboard. It bounces and
speeds across the floor.

The ball is easy to roll, but hard to control.

Marvin jumps on top of it and tries to steer it.

It rolls over and over with Marvin holding on tight. Thank goodness for his hard shell.

"Marvin, watch out!" Elaine cries. "Or that ball will squash you like a bug."

Finally, they reach James's room. It's empty.

They are trying to decide where to put his present when they hear noises in the hallway. James runs in. His arms are full of shopping bags.

Elaine hides behind the leg of the
chair. Marvin gives the super ball a
push. It rolls across the rug.

"Hey!" James cries. "My old
super ball! I thought I lost it."

Ha! This ball must have
belonged to James before James and
Marvin were even friends.

James bounces it high in the air,
catching it. "Cool!"

He spots Marvin and picks him up. "Did you find this? Thanks, little guy," he says.

That makes Marvin happy.

"Want to see my new suit?" James asks.

He opens one of the shopping bags and pulls out a fancy blue suit. It looks like something Mr. Pompaday would wear, not James. But it is small, James's size.

"And here's the best part," James
says. "The tie."

He pulls out a striped tie, then
holds up something little and shiny
for Marvin to see.

It is silver and shaped like a . . .
BEETLE!

"It's called a tie clasp," James says.
"My dad let me pick it out. I'm
going to wear it on my tie at the
wedding."

That makes Marvin *very* happy.

"I really hope you can come with me," James says. "It will make me feel better if you're there."

Marvin hopes he can go to the wedding too . . . and he knows there is someone else who is counting on it.

CHAPTER FOUR
A Wedding Emergency

Finally, it is the morning of the wedding! The weather is warm and sunny. It will be a beautiful day at the Cloisters. James is busy putting on his new suit. Marvin and Elaine

are busy begging their parents to let them go to the wedding.

At first, Mama, Papa, Uncle Albert, and Aunt Edith do not like this idea at all. The wedding is in a strange place, far away.

But Marvin and Elaine remind them that not so long ago, James

saved Uncle Albert's life. And now
he needs them.

"Without James, my dear father
would be gone," Elaine says sadly.

"Besides," Marvin adds, "we're
always safe with James."

When the grown-ups still can't
decide, Elaine sheds a few tears. "I've

never seen the world," she cries.
"This might be my only chance
before I DIE."

"All right, all right, that's enough,"
Uncle Albert says.

The grown-ups look at each other. "You can go," Papa says finally. "But stay together, and stay out of sight."

"And be back before dinner," Mama adds.

Elaine and Marvin grab each other's front legs and spin in a circle.

"The wedding!" Elaine shouts. "We're going to the wedding!"

When they reach James's room,
he is sitting on his bed in his new
suit, fixing his tie with the silver
beetle tie clasp. Marvin and Elaine
race across the rug to the desk. As
soon as they get to the top, James
spots them.

"Hey, little guy! You're here! And you brought a friend. Does this mean you're coming to the wedding?"

In answer, Marvin and Elaine climb onto his finger.

They hear Karl's voice in the
hallway. "James! It's time."

James smiles and quickly puts
them both in his coat pocket, hidden
behind a handkerchief.

"Ready," he calls back.

And off they go to the wedding.

So many sights and sounds! Marvin and Elaine huddle close in James's pocket, peeking out. They whisper excitedly during the elevator ride downstairs, and on the walk along the street. In the cab to the Cloisters, they sneak out for a better view but then quickly return to their hiding spot.

The city whizzes past.

Inside the cab, Karl is wearing a black tuxedo. Marvin thinks he looks very handsome.

"I've got the ring," Karl tells James, hugging him and smiling. "I'll give it to you right before the wedding starts."

"Okay," James says.

"There's nothing to worry about," Karl says. "You'll hold it for a few minutes, then hand it to me, and then I'll put it on Christina's finger."

James nods, looking serious.

When they get to the Cloisters, the sun is shining and flowers are in bloom all around them. The old stone church is high on a hill. Marvin and Elaine lean over the edge of James's pocket. They can see everything, even the big Hudson River, shining far below.

"Where's Christina?" James asks.

"We won't see her until the music starts," Karl tells him. "She wants her wedding dress to be a surprise."

They walk quickly through crowds of people, under stone arches, past

statues, and into a courtyard filled
with flowers. White chairs are set
up in two rows. There are four
people playing music in the corner.
Mr. and Mrs. Pompaday and William
are already there.

Mrs. Pompaday rushes over, holding William. "Oh, James, don't you look nice. We'll be right here in the second row, to see you be the best man! And then you'll come home with us when everything is over."

"Ya ya!" William yells.

Marvin can tell James is glad to see them, but there's no time to talk.

James and Karl hurry to stand in front of everyone.

"Stay out of sight," Marvin reminds Elaine.

They peek out at the people, the flowers, and the tall stone walls of the church. Marvin sees that the stones are very old. He wonders if there were other weddings inside this church, hundreds of years ago, across the ocean in France.

"I can't wait to see the bride,"
Elaine whispers.

"James," Karl says, "here is the
ring." He takes a small gold band out

of a box and hands it to James. "Give
it back to me in a few minutes when
I ask."

"Okay," James says. Marvin can see
that James is nervous.

Karl squeezes his shoulder.
"You're the BEST best man any guy
could ask for."

As James smiles up at his dad, the
music starts.

And then Christina appears. She
is wearing a long white dress. Her
hair is in a bun. She is carrying a big
bouquet of flowers. She walks across
the courtyard to Karl and James, her
face glowing.

"Oh," Elaine says, "she looks
beautiful!"

The music stops, and a woman
in a suit stands between Karl and
Christina. She starts talking about
love and family and getting married.

"They're in LOVE," Elaine
whispers to Marvin. "And now they
are going to be together forever."

Marvin knows this isn't always
true. James's own father and mother,
Karl and Mrs. Pompaday, got married
a long time ago, and they didn't stay
together forever.

But when they got married,
Marvin thinks, they must have *meant*
to stay together forever. And they
had James, who would never have
been born otherwise. Marvin
cannot bear to picture a world
without James.

He is thinking all these things
when he hears Christina cry, "Oh!"

There, in her pretty bunch of
flowers, Marvin sees a bee.

He sees the bee just as Karl asks
James for the ring. And just as James
is handing Karl the ring, two more
bees land in Christina's flowers.

Karl tries to wave them away.

"She's allergic!" he cries.

But the bees keep buzzing around
the flowers.

"Oh no!" Elaine whispers to
Marvin. "This is bad!"

"We have to do something,"
Marvin says.

Together, he and Elaine lean over
the edge of James's pocket, waving
their legs at the bees.

"Hey!" Elaine yells. "Beat it!"

"Please," Marvin calls. "And take your friends with you."

Christina looks frightened. She is waving the bunch of flowers in the air, trying to get rid of the bees.

"What's up?" says one bee, flying near Marvin.

"This is a wedding," Marvin says.
"Please go bother somebody else."

"I'm not bothering anybody," says
the bee. "I'm collecting pollen."

"We know," Elaine says, "but
you're scaring the bride."

"There are flowers all over," Marvin tells him. "Can't you leave this bunch alone?"

The bee sighs. "Okay, okay. But we weren't going to hurt anyone."

The bees take off, just as Christina shakes the bunch of flowers one last time.

And then something truly terrible happens.

Christina's hand hits Karl's hand, and the gold ring he is holding falls through the air.

Marvin freezes.

Elaine gasps.

The ring drops to the stone floor of the courtyard. It bounces once, twice, and then rolls into a metal grate, out of sight.

CHAPTER FIVE
The Ring

"The ring!" Elaine cries. "They can't have a wedding without a ring!"

Marvin barely has time to think. He grabs Elaine's front leg, and together they jump out of James's pocket, after the ring.

They tumble through the air . . .

over and over . . .

. . . until they land on the hard

stones with a *smack*!

It's a good thing they have their

beetle shells to protect them.

They rush to the metal grate.

But it's too late. The ring is gone.

"Oh, Karl," Christina cries. "I'm so sorry! I was trying to get rid of the bees."

"Don't worry," Karl says. "It went into that drain. We'll get it back."

Karl and James drop to the ground, peering into the grate. Marvin and Elaine hide behind a large pebble.

Nobody knows what to do. The
ring has disappeared into a black hole.

Karl tries to lift the grate, but it
is screwed on tight. He shines his
cell-phone light into the blackness
of the drain, but there's nothing
to see. Someone leaves to get a
museum guard.

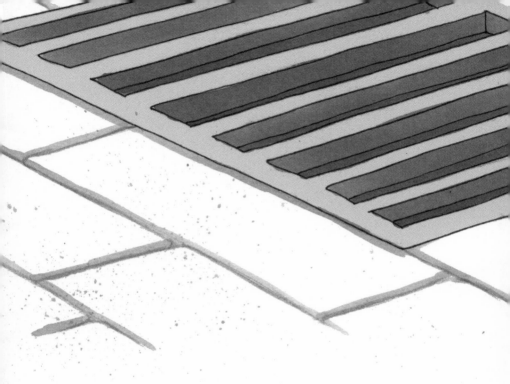

"We have to find that ring," Elaine says to Marvin.

Marvin nods. "Let's go."

They are about to jump into the grate when James sees them.

Quickly, he covers them with his hand. Now they can't go anywhere.

James turns to Karl. "Maybe I can

fit my finger in there. I can try to
reach the ring."

"The gaps are so small," Karl says.
"I don't want your finger to get
stuck."

"Please don't take any chances,"
Christina says.

"Let me try," James tells them.

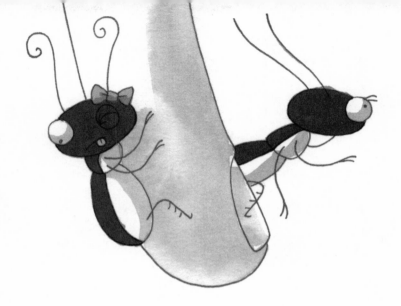

He bends over the grate and sticks his pointer finger into the drain.

Marvin sees their chance. "Now," he says to Elaine, and together, they run along the inside of James's finger until they are below the grate, inside the dark drain hole.

Clinging to James's finger, they look around.

The drain is not very deep. At
first, all Marvin can see are the
metal walls of a pipe and little piles
of leaves and twigs.

"Yuck," Elaine says. "It's dirty
down here. Do you see the ring?"

"No," Marvin says.

They peer through the darkness.
Luckily, beetles have excellent night
vision. They don't need a light to see
anything down here.

And then Marvin *does* see
something. A flash of gold. "Elaine,
over there!"

"The ring!" Elaine cries. "We found it!" She drops off James's fingertip to the bottom of the shallow drain and rushes to the spot where the ring has fallen.

She tries to lift it. "Ugh, it's too heavy," Elaine says.

Marvin jumps down beside her.

Even working together, they cannot lift that heavy ring. And James's finger is too short to reach it.

"I know," Marvin says. "We can roll it." So that is what they do. They roll the ring directly under James's fingertip.

But just then, James pulls his
finger back up into the world above.

For a minute Marvin is scared.
What is going on? Is James leaving
them down here?

Then he hears James's voice. "I
think I see it."

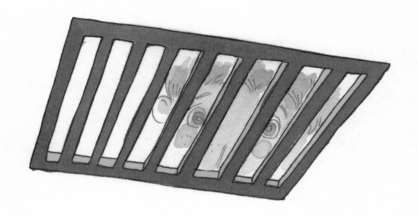

Other voices say, "Really?"

"You do?"

"James found the ring!"

Marvin and Elaine look up, and
James's big eyes look down at them
through the metal bars of the grate.
"I don't think I can reach it," he says.
"Hang on . . ."

The next thing they know, James's two fingers are poking through the grate, holding something long and silver.

The beetle tie clasp!

Now there are *three* beetles in the drain.

James pinches the tie clasp open and waves it in the air above them.

They duck.

"Yikes," Elaine says. "That thing is sharp."

"We have to hold the ring where he can grab it," Marvin says.

They stand on either side of the ring, and with all their might, they try to lift it. It is so heavy. *Oomph!*

Finally, they raise it up, just enough to bang the tie clasp with a *clink.*

The tie clasp closes on the ring, and—*hooray!*—James lifts it out of the drain.

Above ground, what a commotion there is! Marvin and Elaine can hear everyone cheering and clapping for James.

"Let's get out of here," Elaine says. "Or we'll miss the wedding!"

They crawl up the slippery side of the pipe and through the grate.

James is there, watching for them. Grinning, he quickly bends down to

tie his shoe. He sweeps Marvin and
Elaine into his hand and tucks them
both back in the pocket of his suit
jacket.

"You did great, little guy," he
whispers. "And your friend too."

Marvin and Elaine beam at each
other. They saved the day!

The bees are gone. The ring is back. Everything is just as it should be, and now it's time for the wedding.

Karl says, "With this ring, I thee wed." He slides the golden ring onto Christina's finger.

Marvin and Elaine stay hidden in
James's pocket.

Elaine sniffles. "It's so beautiful."

"What?" Marvin asks.

"Love!" She turns to Marvin.

"Marvin, you did it. You found the ring."

"*We* did it," Marvin says. "And James helped. James always helps."

"That's what friends are for," Elaine says.